PUSS IN BOOTS
AND OTHER STORIES

PUSS IN BOOTS

AND OTHER STORIES

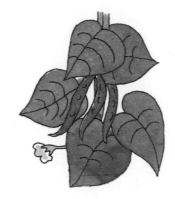

TOLD AND ILLUSTRATED BY

ANNE ROCKWELL

MACMILLAN PUBLISHING COMPANY   NEW YORK
COLLIER MACMILLAN PUBLISHERS   LONDON

FOR PHYLLIS

Printed and bound in Japan
First American Edition   10 9 8 7 6 5 4 3 2 1

The text of this book is set in 14 point Trump Medieval.
The illustrations are serigraphs hand painted in watercolor and gouache.

Library of Congress Cataloging-in-Publication Data
Rockwell, Anne F. Puss in boots and other stories. Summary: A collection of traditional stories including "Jack and the Beanstalk," "The Fisherman and His Wife," and "Briar Rose." 1. Fairy tales. [1. Fairy tales. 2. Folklore] I. Title. PZ8.R616Pu 1988 398.1'1 87-14976
ISBN 0-02-777781-2

CONTENTS

AUTHOR'S NOTE

THESE stories are very, very old. No one knows where they were first told, or when, or by whom. Before there were any books to read, they were told in cold stone castle halls, to families sitting around dimly flickering cottage fires, and to crowds gathered in village markets. Down through the centuries, generation after generation, each storyteller told the old stories for new listeners much as he or she remembered them. But, at the same time, each storyteller brought something of himself or herself to the traditional tales, and I have tried to do the same.

The versions I have based my tellings on are usually those I knew in my childhood, versions in long-lost storybooks, which were in turn based upon the work of such storytellers as the brothers Grimm, Charles Perrault, Joseph Jacobs, Aesop, Asbjörnsen and Moe, La Fontaine, and others who wrote down the stories as they heard them in their own times. I have tried to give each story the sparkle I remember so well from the very first time I heard it.

These stories have lived so long, I think, partly because they tell us, over and over again, that our actions have consequences. It is always very satisfying to see that each story ends exactly as we know it should. Good and kind people are *always* rewarded, while foolish or evil folk *always* get what they have coming to them, too. If you are selfish, cruel, or foolish, you will suffer for it, but if you are kind, brave, generous, loyal, and clever, you will certainly be rewarded, usually in very surprising ways.

The world of these stories is often controlled by the very special folk of fairy tales—Wise Women, gnomes, fairies, ogres, witches, trolls, or enchanted beasts—who are gifted in magic and use it as they wish. These magical beings can be good or evil. Sometimes, in fact, the good-hearted and brave have to use clever tricks in order to outwit cruel and monstrous magical beings, as Jack, for example, does with the ogre at the top of the wonderful beanstalk.

I love these stories. They were read to me when I was little, and, as soon as I could read, I read them over to myself. I read them later to my own children, and they reread them, just as I had done. I hope you will enjoy them, too.

JACK
AND THE
BEANSTALK

THERE was once a poor widow who had a son named Jack and a cow named Milky White. All they had to live on was the milk the cow gave every morning, which they sold in the market. But at last Milky White gave no more milk, and they didn't know what to do.

"Cheer up, Mother. I'll go and get work somewhere," said Jack.

"We tried that before, and no one would hire you," said Jack's mother. "We will have to sell Milky White and start a shop with the money."

"All right, Mother," said Jack. "Today is market day. I'll soon sell Milky White, and then we'll see what we can do."

So off Jack went, leading Milky White to market. He hadn't gone far when he met a funny-looking old man who said to him, "Good morning, Jack."

"Good morning to you," said Jack, and wondered how the man knew his name.

"Where are you off to?" asked the man.

"I'm going to market to sell our cow," said Jack.

"You look smart enough to sell a cow," said the man. "I wonder if you can tell me how many beans make five?"

"Two in each hand and one in your mouth," Jack answered him.

"Right you are," said the man, "and here they are, the very beans themselves." As he spoke, he pulled a handful of odd-looking beans out of his pocket. "Since you are so smart," he said, "I don't mind swapping your cow for these beans."

"I'm smart enough to know my cow is worth more than your beans," said Jack.

"Ah! You don't know what wonderful beans these are," said the man. "Plant them tonight. By morning they will grow right up into the sky."

"Really?" said Jack.

"Yes, and if it doesn't turn out to be true, you can have your cow back," said the man.

"Well, that's fair enough," said Jack. So he gave Milky White to the funny-looking old man and put the beans in his pocket.

When Jack got home and told his mother that he had sold Milky White for a handful of beans, she was so angry she threw the beans out the window. Then she sent Jack to bed without any supper.

So Jack went upstairs to his little room in the attic. He was sad and sorry because his mother was angry at him and he had gotten no supper.

At last he dropped off to sleep.

When he woke, his room looked very strange. The sun was shining into part of it, while the rest was quite dark. Jack jumped up and went to his window. What do you think he saw? Why, those beans his mother had thrown out the window had sprung up into a great, huge beanstalk. It went up and up until it reached the sky. So the funny-looking old man had told the truth.

The beanstalk grew close to the house, so Jack opened his window and jumped onto the beanstalk. He began to climb it, and he climbed and he climbed until, at last, he reached the sky. When he got there he found a long, straight road. Jack walked along the long, straight road until he came to a big, tall house. On the doorstep stood a big, tall woman.

"Good morning, ma'am," said Jack, politely. "Would you be so kind as to give me some breakfast?"

"It's breakfast you want, is it?" said the big, tall woman. "It's breakfast you'll be if you don't get out of here. My man is an ogre, and there's nothing he likes better than boys broiled on toast. You'd better move on, for he'll soon be coming home."

"Oh, please, ma'am, do give me something to eat. I've had nothing to eat since yesterday morning. I might as well be broiled as die of hunger," said Jack.

Well, the ogre's wife was not so bad, after all. She took Jack into the kitchen and gave him a chunk of bread and a pitcher of milk. But Jack wasn't half-finished when the whole house began to tremble with the noise of someone coming.

"Goodness, gracious me! It's my husband," said the ogre's wife. "Come along—quick—and jump in here." And she shoved Jack into the oven just as the ogre walked in.

He was a big one, to be sure. At his belt hung

three oxen. He threw them down on the table and said, "Here, Wife, broil me a couple of these for breakfast. Ah! What is this I smell?

"*Fee-fi-fo-fum,*
   I smell the blood of an Englishman.
   Be he live or be he dead
   I'll grind his bones to make my bread!"

"Nonsense, my dearie," said his wife. "You're dreaming. Or perhaps you smell the scraps of that little boy you had for yesterday's dinner. You go wash up, and by the time you come back your breakfast will be ready."

So off the ogre went. Jack was just going to jump out of the oven and run home when the woman said, "Wait until he is asleep. He always has a snooze after breakfast."

The ogre ate his breakfast. After that he went to a big chest and took out two bags of gold coins. He sat down and began to count his gold. He counted and counted until his head began to nod. Soon he began to snore until the whole house shook.

Jack crept out of the oven. As he passed the sleeping ogre, he grabbed one of the bags of gold.

Then off he ran until he came to the beanstalk. He threw down the bag of gold, which landed right in his mother's garden. And he climbed down, down, down, until at last he got home.

He showed his mother the bag of gold and said, "Well, Mother, wasn't I right about the beans? They were really magic, you see."

Jack and his mother used the gold coins to buy their food for some time. But at last they had spent all of them. So Jack decided to try his luck again at the top of the beanstalk.

One fine morning he rose early, and he climbed and he climbed until he reached the sky.

There was the same long, straight road and the same big, tall house. Sure enough, the same big, tall woman was standing on the doorstep.

"Good morning, ma'am," said Jack. "Could you give me something to eat?"

"Go away, my boy," said the big, tall woman, "or else my man will eat you for breakfast. Tell me, aren't you the boy who came here before? Do you know, that very day my husband couldn't find one of his bags of gold."

"That's strange, ma'am," said Jack. "I might be able to tell you something about that, but I'm so hungry I can't speak until I've had some breakfast."

The big, tall woman was so curious that she took Jack in and give him some bread and milk. He had scarcely begun eating when they heard the ogre's footsteps and his wife hid Jack in the oven.

All happened as it had before. In came the ogre, carrying three oxen. He said,

"Fee-fi-fo-fum,
I smell the blood of an Englishman.
Be he live or be he dead
I'll grind his bones to make my bread!"

When he had eaten his breakfast he said, "Wife, bring me the hen that lays the golden eggs."

She brought it, and the ogre said, "Lay!" and the hen laid an egg of pure gold. Then the ogre began to nod his head. Soon he was snoring until the house shook and rattled.

Jack crept out of the oven and grabbed the hen and ran. But this time the hen gave a cackle that woke the ogre. Just as Jack got out of the house, he heard the ogre calling, "Wife! Wife! What have you done with my hen that lays the golden eggs?"

His wife said, "Why do you ask, my dearie?"

And that was all Jack heard, for he was climbing down the beanstalk as fast as he could go.

When he got home he showed his mother the wonderful hen and said, "Lay!" and it laid a golden egg. Every time he said "Lay!" the hen laid another golden egg. Then they sold the eggs for money to buy food.

But Jack was not content with this. It wasn't very long before he made up his mind to try his luck again at the top of the beanstalk. So one fine morning he rose up early, and he climbed and he climbed until he reached the sky.

This time he knew better than to go straight to the ogre's house. When he got near it, he hid behind a bush until he saw the ogre's wife come out to fetch some water. Then he crept into the house and hid in the soup pot.

He hadn't been there long before he heard the ogre's heavy footsteps thumping through the house. In came the ogre and his wife.

"Fee-fi-fo-fum! I smell the blood of an English-man!" said the ogre. "I smell him, Wife, I do!"

"Do you, my dearie?" said the ogre's wife. "If it is that naughty boy who stole your bag of gold and your hen that lays the golden eggs, he is sure to be hiding in the oven." They both rushed to the oven. But Jack wasn't there, luckily for him.

So the ogre's wife said, "Why don't you just eat your nice breakfast, my dearie?"

The ogre sat down and ate his breakfast. But every now and then he would mutter, "Well, I could have sworn . . ." and he would get up and search in all the cabinets and everywhere else. Fortunately, he didn't think to look inside the soup pot.

After he had eaten breakfast the ogre said, "Wife, bring me my golden harp." So she brought it to the table. He said, "Sing!" and the golden harp sang most beautifully. It went on singing until the ogre fell asleep and began to snore like thunder.

Then, very quietly, Jack lifted up the lid of the soup pot and tiptoed to the table. He grabbed the golden harp and ran toward the door as fast as he could go. But the harp cried out quite loudly, "Master! Master!" and the ogre woke up just in time to see Jack running away with his harp.

Jack ran as fast as he could, and the ogre came rushing after him. When Jack got to the beanstalk, the ogre was not more than twenty yards behind him.

Suddenly the ogre saw Jack disappear. He was very surprised when he got to the end of the road and saw Jack climbing down the beanstalk. Well, the ogre was so big and heavy that he felt a bit nervous at the thought of climbing down the beanstalk. He waited a few moments to summon up his courage. So Jack was able to get ahead of him.

But suddenly the harp called out again, "Master! Master!" and the ogre swung himself onto the beanstalk. It swayed and swayed with all that weight. Down climbed Jack, and after him climbed the ogre. Down, down went Jack until he was nearly home. Then he shouted, "Mother! Mother! Bring me the ax!"

His mother came rushing out of the house with the ax in her hand. When she saw the ogre coming down the beanstalk after Jack and heard the golden harp crying "Master! Master!" she froze with fright.

Jack jumped to the ground and grabbed the ax. He gave a good chop to the beanstalk. Then he gave another good chop with his ax and another and another until the beanstalk toppled over. The ogre fell to the ground, and that was the end of him.

Jack gave the golden harp to his mother. Soon people came from near and far to hear the harp sing. With the money they made from that and from the hen that laid the golden eggs, Jack and his mother grew very rich, and they lived happily ever after.

THERE was once a tramp who was traveling through a forest at night. Suddenly he saw a little cottage. Smoke was coming from the chimney. How nice it would be to sit in front of a warm fire and have a bite of something to eat, he thought. So he knocked at the door of the cottage.

"Good evening, and well met," he said to the woman who came to the door.

"Good evening," said the woman, crossly. "Where do you come from?"

"South of the sun and east of the moon," said the tramp. "I have been all over the world, and now I am on my way home again."

"And what is your business here?" said the woman.

"Oh, I want only a shelter for the night," he said.

"I thought so," said the woman. "You might as well be on your way. My husband is not at home, and my house is not an inn."

"My good woman," said the tramp, "you must not be so cross and hard-hearted. We are both human beings, and we should help one another."

"Help one another? Help?" said the woman. "I never heard of such nonsense. Who will help me, I wonder. I haven't a thing to eat in the house. No, you'll have to look for shelter elsewhere."

He went on begging her for shelter for the night, and she went on grumbling and complaining, but at last the woman gave in and told the tramp he could sleep on her floor that night.

The tramp thanked her kindly and said, "Better the floor with no sleep than freeze in the forest deep!" for he was a cheerful fellow who was always ready with a rhyme.

When the tramp came inside the cottage, he could see that the woman was not as poor as she pretended to be.

Instead, she was a greedy and stingy person of a sort he had often met in his travels. He made himself very agreeable and asked her in his most polite and pleasant manner for something to eat.

"Where am I to get it from?" said the woman. "I haven't had a morsel myself all day."

But that tramp was a clever fellow, he was.

"Poor thing! You must be starving," he said. "Well, I suppose I will have to ask you to have something with me, then."

"Have something with you?" said the woman. "You don't look as if you could have anything to offer me. What have you got, I'd like to know?"

"He who far and wide does roam learns many things not known at home," said the tramp. "Lend me a pot and spoon, if you please."

Now the woman became very curious, so she loaned him a pot and spoon. He filled the pot with water and put it on the fire. He blew with all his might until the fire blazed nicely around it. Then he took a four-inch nail from his pocket and put it in the pot. The woman stared and stared.

"What is this going to be?" she asked.

"Nail soup," said the tramp, stirring the water that was boiling in the pot.

"Nail soup?" said the woman.

"Yes, nail soup," said the tramp, and went on stirring and humming a little tune as he stirred.

The woman thought she had heard of many strange things in her time, but she had never heard of anyone making soup with a nail before.

"This usually makes excellent soup," said the tramp. "But this time it looks as if it will be rather weak, for I have been making soup for five nights with that one nail. If only I had a cup of oatmeal to put in it, that would thicken it nicely. But what one has to do without it's no use to think about," he said as he took a little taste of the soup.

"Well, I might have a bit of oatmeal somewhere," said the woman, and went to fetch some.

The tramp poured in the oatmeal. He went on stirring and tasting, while the woman stared at him so hard it looked as if her eyes would pop.

"This soup would be good enough for company," he said, "if only I had a bit of salted beef and a few potatoes to put in. But what one has to do without it's no use to think about."

Then the woman remembered that she had a few potatoes and a bit of beef, besides. She gave these to the tramp, who went on stirring, and she sat and stared as hard as ever.

"If only I had a little milk and barley, I could ask the king himself to take a sip," said the tramp. "He has this soup for supper every night. I know this is true, for I used to be servant to the king's own cook."

The woman was so impressed to hear of the tramp's grand connections that she wasted no time finding a pitcher of milk and a cup of barley.

The tramp went on stirring, and the woman went on staring. At last the tramp took a taste and closed his eyes and smiled.

"Now it is ready, and it is just the way the queen likes it best. Of course," he said, "with this kind of soup the king and queen always have a linen cloth on the table and china bowls and silver spoons. But what one has to do without it's no use to think about."

No sooner had he said this than the woman opened her cupboard and took out a fine white linen cloth and china bowls and silver spoons and napkins, too. She set the table and put a good loaf of bread and a big, yellow cheese on the table, and a few pickles, besides. At last the table looked as though it were decked out for company.

The tramp took the nail out of the soup, and he and the woman had a fine feast.

The woman said, "I have never tasted such good soup. And, imagine, all made with a nail!"

She was in such a good and cheerful mood from having learned such an economical way to make soup that she insisted upon making up a warm bed for the tramp to sleep in. The next morning, when he awoke, the first thing he got was hot coffee and a piece of cake. And when he was ready to leave, the woman gave him a silver coin to see him on his way.

"Many thanks for what you have taught me," she said to the tramp. "Now I shall live in comfort for the rest of my days, since I have learned to make soup with a nail."

And the tramp went whistling on his way.

KATE
CRACKERNUTS

THERE once lived a king and a queen. The king had a daughter of his own named Anne, and the queen had a daughter of her own named Kate. Anne was much prettier than Kate. All the same, the two girls loved each other like real sisters, and only the queen was jealous because the king's daughter was so much prettier than her own child. She began to think of ways to spoil Anne's beauty.

Not far from the castle there lived an old henwife who raised chickens and knew much magic, besides. One day the queen went to her for advice. The henwife said, "Send the girl to me tomorrow morning, but make sure she comes with nothing to eat."

Before breakfast the queen said to Anne, "Go, my dear, to the henwife in the glen and ask her for some eggs." Anne set out right away, but as she passed through the kitchen, she saw a crust of bread. She picked it up and munched it as she walked.

When Anne came to the henwife's, she asked for eggs as she had been told to do. The henwife said to her, "Lift the lid off the pot and you'll see." The girl did so, but nothing happened.

"Go home to your mother and tell her to keep her larder door better locked," said the henwife.

So Anne went home to the queen and told her what the henwife had said. The queen knew from this that the pretty princess had eaten something before she had seen the henwife.

The next morning the queen again sent Anne to fetch eggs from the henwife. She watched very carefully to make sure that Anne had nothing to eat before setting out, but on the way the princess saw some people picking peas by the roadside. She stopped and spoke to them, and they offered her a handful of peas, which she munched along the way.

When she got to the henwife's and asked for eggs, the henwife said, "Lift the lid off the pot and you'll see." Anne lifted the lid, but nothing happened. Then the henwife was angry and said to Anne, "Tell your mother the pot won't boil if the fire's away." So Anne went home and told the queen.

The third day the queen went with the girl to the henwife to make sure she ate nothing. And this time when Anne lifted the lid off the pot, her own pretty face vanished. In its place was a sheep's head.

At this the queen was quite satisfied, and she and Anne went home.

When Kate saw Anne with a sheep's head where her own pretty face had been, she wanted to help her. So she took fine linen cloth and made a veil to cover her sister's face, and they both went out into the world.

They walked on and on until they came to a castle. Kate knocked at the door and asked for a night's lodging for herself and her sister. When they went inside, they found that it was a king's castle.

Now this king had two sons. One of them was very sick, and no one could find out what was wrong with him. The curious thing was that whoever nursed the sick prince through the night was never seen again. The king had offered a peck of silver to anyone who would sit up with him all night. Kate was a very brave girl, so she offered to sit up with the king's sick son.

Until midnight all went well. But at twelve o'clock the sick prince rose from his bed. He dressed himself and slipped downstairs. Kate followed him, but he didn't seem to notice her. The prince went to his stable, saddled his horse, and called his hound. When he mounted his horse, Kate leaped up lightly behind him.

Away rode the prince with Kate sitting behind

him. As they rode through the wood, Kate picked nuts from the trees above and filled her apron with them. They rode on and on until they came to a green hill.

The prince said, "Open, open, green hill, and let the young prince in with his horse and hound." Kate added, "And his lady behind him."

Immediately the green hill opened, and they rode in. Just inside was a magnificent hall, brightly lit and filled with fairies dancing. Some of the fairies surrounded the prince and led him off to join the dance. Kate hid herself behind the door and watched. The prince danced and danced through the night. Whenever he could dance no longer, he would fall down upon a couch. Then the fairies would fan him until he rose again to dance some more.

At last the cock crowed, and the prince made haste to get on his horse. Kate jumped up behind him, and home they rode.

When the morning sun arose, the king came in and saw the prince sleeping and Kate sitting by the fire cracking the nuts she had gathered in the wood. Kate said the prince had passed a good night, but she would not sit up another night with him unless she got a peck of gold.

The second night passed as had the first. The prince got up at midnight and rode away to the green hill and the fairy ball. Kate went with him, gathering nuts as they rode through the wood. This time she could not bear to watch the prince, for she knew he would dance and dance until he dropped.

From her hiding place Kate saw a fairy baby playing with a wand and overheard one of the fairies say,

"Three taps of that wand would make Kate's sister as pretty as she ever was." So Kate rolled her nuts to the fairy baby until the baby toddled after the nuts and dropped the wand. Kate picked up the wand and hid it in her apron.

When the cock crowed, Kate and the prince rode home as before. The moment she got home Kate rushed to her room and tapped Anne three times with the wand. As soon as she did so, the ugly sheep's head vanished, and Anne was her own pretty self again.

The third night Kate told the king she would watch over the sick prince only if she could marry him. All happened as it had the first two nights.

This time the fairy baby was playing with a little bird. Kate heard one of the fairies say, "Three bites of that birdie would make the sick prince as well as he ever was." Kate rolled all the nuts she had to the fairy baby until it dropped the bird, and Kate hid it in her apron.

As soon as the cock crowed, Kate and the prince set off again. When they reached the castle, Kate killed the bird, plucked its feathers, and roasted it over the fire in the prince's room. It smelled most delicious.

The sick prince woke up and moaned most pitifully, "Oh, if only I had a bite of that birdie!" When Kate gave him a bite of the roasted bird—just one tiny bite—the prince pulled himself up from his pillow and rested on his elbow. He begged for another bite, and so Kate gave him one. Then he sat straight up in bed and cried, "Oh, if only I could have a third bite of that delicious birdie!"

After the third bite the prince got up out of his bed and stretched himself and went to the window and smiled at the rising sun. Then he sat down cheerfully by the fire with Kate, for now the dreadful fairy spell was broken and he was his own strong, healthy, and friendly self again.

When the king and his folk came in to see how the prince was feeling, they were amazed to see him sitting by the fire with Kate, cracking nuts and laughing merrily as they talked. Meanwhile, the prince's brother had seen pretty Anne and fallen in love with her, as did everyone who saw her sweet face. So the prince who had been enchanted married Kate, and his brother married Anne. Then they all lived happily ever after.

THE MILLER,
HIS SON, AND
THE DONKEY

THERE once lived a miller and his young son who were taking their donkey to market to sell it. Along the way they met a group of girls laughing and talking.

The girls said, "Did you ever see such a couple of fools? Why do they trudge along the hot and dusty road when they could ride in comfort?"

The miller thought there was good sense in what they said. He told his son to get on the donkey's back, and he walked along by his side.

By and by they met some old friends of the miller. They greeted him and then said, "You'll spoil that lazy boy of yours if you don't look out. Imagine letting him ride in comfort while you walk on foot. Make him walk! It will do him good."

So the miller followed their advice and took his son's place on the donkey's back. They had not gone far before they passed a group of children.

The miller heard them say, "What a selfish old man! He rides along in comfort while his poor son has to drag himself along the road." This time the miller told his son to climb up behind him.

By and by they met some travelers. They asked the miller whether the donkey was his own or one he had hired for the day. The miller proudly told them it was his very own donkey and he was taking it to market to sell.

They said, "For goodness' sake! With a heavy load like that, the poor beast will be so tired by the time he gets to market that no one will buy him. You'd do better to carry him!"

"You might be right," said the miller. "We can try that." So he and his son got off and tied the donkey's legs together with a rope. Then they slung him upside down on a pole.

At last they came to town, carrying the donkey between them. This was such a funny sight that people ran out in crowds to look at them. All the people laughed and jeered at the father and son and called them crazy folk.

When the miller and his son were going across a bridge over a river, the donkey was so frightened by the noise of all the people laughing and jeering, not to speak of being carried upside down on a pole, that he began to kick and hee-haw and struggle. At last the poor donkey kicked so hard that he broke the rope that tied him to the pole and fell into the river and drowned.

The unhappy miller and his son made their way home that evening as best they could. They were very distressed to see that by trying to please everyone they had pleased no one and had lost their donkey in the bargain.

THERE was once a man who had three sons. The two oldest boys were clever fellows, and their parents were very proud of them. But the youngest was called Dummling because he was not as smart as his brothers. Everyone made fun of him, and his mother and father were ashamed of him because they believed he was stupid.

One day the oldest son wanted to go into the forest to chop some wood. Before he went, his mother baked him a delicious sweet cake and gave him a bottle of wine so that he would not get hungry or thirsty as he worked in the forest.

Not long after he entered the forest, he met a little gray man who said to him, "Please give me a piece of your cake and let me have a sip of your wine. I am so hungry and thirsty."

The clever son said, "If I give you some of my cake and wine, I will not have much left for myself.

Be off with you!" And he left the little gray man and went on his way.

But no sooner had he begun to chop down a tree than his ax slipped and he cut his arm. He had to go home and have it bandaged up. This was the little gray man's doing.

Then the second son went into the forest to chop wood. His mother gave him a sweet cake and a bottle of wine just as she had his brother. He had not gone far when he met the same little gray man. The little man asked the second brother for a piece of cake and a drink of wine, just as he had the first.

The second son answered, sensibly enough, "What I give to you will be taken from me. Be off!" And he left the little man and went on his way.

Now, that little gray man knew powerful magic. So after the second brother made a few chops at the tree, he cut himself in the leg and had to go home and have it bandaged.

Then Dummling said, "Father, let me go and cut some wood. I want to be a help to you."

His father said, "Your brothers are smarter than you are, and they are good at things you cannot do. Yet look at how they have hurt themselves chopping wood. You had better stay home, for you don't know anything about it and you are clumsy and stupid, besides."

But Dummling begged for so long that at last his father said, "Oh, go off to the forest, then. But don't blame me if you hurt yourself. Perhaps you will learn a lesson from it if you do!" His mother gave him a cake made with water and baked in cinders and a bottle of sour beer for his lunch.

When Dummling entered the forest, the little gray man came up to him, just as he had to his brothers. The man said, "Give me a piece of your cake and a drink from your bottle. I am so hungry and thirsty."

Dummling answered, "I have only cinder cake and sour beer, but if you would like some we can sit down and eat."

They sat down in the quiet forest together, and Dummling opened the sack that held his lunch. Then a very strange thing happened. As Dummling offered half of his cinder cake to the little gray man he saw that it had become a fine, sweet cake and the sour beer had become good, cool wine. They both ate and drank a very fine lunch.

When they had finished the little gray man said,

"Since you have a kind heart and are willing to share what you have, I will give you some good luck. Cut down that old tree over there and see what you will find at the roots." Then the little gray man vanished into the forest.

Dummling did as he was told and cut down the tree. He did not hurt himself as his brothers had done. When the tree fell over on the forest floor, Dummling saw sitting in its roots a goose with shining feathers of the purest gold.

Dummling decided the time had come to travel and see what else there was in the wide world. He lifted up the golden goose and took her with him.

That night Dummling stopped at an inn. The innkeeper had three daughters. As soon as they saw the goose, each daughter wanted one of its golden feathers for herself.

The oldest daughter watched and waited until Dummling had gone out of the room. Then she grabbed the golden goose by its wing, but instead of pulling out a feather her hand stuck fast to the goose. No matter how hard she tried to pull it away, her hand only stuck harder.

The innkeeper's second daughter came soon after to get a golden feather from the goose. She tried to push her sister out of the way, so she could pull out a feather. But no sooner had she touched her sister's shoulder than she stuck to her, just as her sister had stuck to the goose.

At last the third sister came. Her sisters screamed out, "Keep away! For goodness' sake, keep away!" But she did not understand why, and she ran to them. She wanted to push her sisters away from the golden goose. But no sooner had she touched the second sister than she, too, stuck fast. So all three sisters had to spend the night with the goose.

The next morning Dummling took the golden goose under his arm and set out on his way. The three girls who were stuck to the goose had to run after him wherever his legs went.

In the middle of a field the parson met them. When he saw the procession he said, "Shame on you, girls! Why are you chasing after this young man?" As he spoke the parson pulled the third sister by the hand to get her away from Dummling and his goose. But then the parson, too, stuck fast. So he had to run behind Dummling, the golden goose, and the three daughters of the innkeeper.

While the five of them were trotting along, one behind the other, the parson shouted out to two laborers to help him. One laborer grabbed the parson's arm while the other—a big, strong fellow—tried to pull the parson loose by tugging him around the middle. But the laborers stuck to the parson, who was stuck to the third sister, who was stuck to the second, who was stuck to the first, who was stuck to the golden goose that Dummling was carrying.

Soon Dummling came to a city. The king who ruled over that city had a daughter who was so sad and serious that she never laughed at anything, no matter how funny. The king had put forth a decree stating that whoever could make his daughter laugh would be able to marry her.

Dummling came down the road just under the palace window, carrying his goose. All the people who were stuck to it were following along behind him wherever his legs would go. The princess happened to be gazing soberly out the window just at that very moment. When she saw the people running along, one stuck to the other, she began to laugh. She laughed some more. And before long she was laughing as if she would never stop.

When Dummling heard about the king's decree, he went to the king and asked for the princess to be his wife. But the king did not want a fellow who was believed to be stupid for his son-in-law. So he added another condition that had to be met before Dummling could marry his daughter. He said that unless Dummling could find someone who could drink a cellar full of wine in one day, the wedding could not take place.

Dummling thought of the little gray man and went into the forest to try to find him. In the very spot where he had chopped down the tree that held the golden goose, he saw a man sitting with a most sad and miserable expression on his face.

When Dummling asked him why he was so sad, the man said, "I have such a terrible thirst! I cannot quench it. I have just emptied a barrel of wine, but to me that is just like a drop on a hot stone."

"I can help you," said Dummling. "Come with me, and you will have plenty to drink."

He led the thirsty man to the king's cellar. The man bent over the huge barrels and began to drink. He drank and drank, and before the day was done he had emptied every barrel.

Then Dummling went to ask the king for his bride. The king was so angry that Dummling had found a man who could drink a cellar full of wine that he made yet another condition.

"Find me a man who can eat a whole mountain of bread in one day," said the king. "Then you can marry my daughter."

Dummling thought again of his friend, the little gray man. He went straight back to the forest, to the very same place where he had cut down the tree.

There he saw a man with an expression of terrible suffering on his face, who groaned and said, "I have eaten a whole oven full of bread, but what good is that when one is as hungry as I am?"

Dummling said to the man, "Get up and come with me. I know a place where you can eat yourself full." He led him to the king's palace, where all the flour in the whole kingdom had been collected and all the bakers in the kingdom had been baking loaf after loaf of bread. In the courtyard stood a huge mountain of bread.

The man from the forest walked up to it and began to eat. By the end of the day the whole mountain of bread had vanished.

For the third time Dummling asked for his bride, and for the third time the king tried to find a way out. At last he said he wanted a ship that could sail on land and water. "As soon as you sail it back to me," he said, "you shall have my daughter for your wife."

Dummling went straight to the forest again. There sat the little gray man to whom he had given his cinder cake and sour beer. When the little man heard what Dummling wanted, he said, "Since you have shared food and drink with me, I will give you a ship that can sail on land and water. I do all this for you because you were good to me." And the little gray man gave Dummling exactly what he wanted.

When Dummling came back to the palace in the ship that could sail on land and water, the king saw that he could no longer prevent the wedding. So Dummling and the princess were married. After the king died Dummling became king, and he ruled with justice and kindness for a long, long time.

THE BOY
WHO CRIED
WOLF

THERE was once a shepherd boy who, day after day, tended his sheep in a meadow that lay between a dark forest and a village. One day the boy thought, Nothing interesting ever happens. Every day is the same. The sheep graze and I sit, day in, day out. I wish something exciting would happen.

Then the boy had an idea. He would pretend that a wolf had come out of the dark forest to eat the sheep. So he ran toward the village, crying "Wolf! Wolf!" as loudly as he could. Every person in the village stopped working and ran with the shepherd boy to chase away the wolf. When they saw no wolf, they believed it had gone back into the woods of its own accord. They were happy to see the sheep were safe, and they went back to their work. No one guessed the boy was fooling them.

A few days later the boy grew bored again. He remembered how exciting it had been when all the people of the village had come rushing to the meadow. So he ran into the village once more, crying "Wolf! Wolf!" Once again everyone came to chase the wolf away from the sheep.

But this time, when the people saw no wolf, they knew that the boy had not been telling the truth when he cried "Wolf! Wolf!" They were all very angry.

Not long after this, a real wolf did come out of the dark forest and began to chase the sheep. The shepherd boy could not stop it. He ran into the village, crying "Wolf! Wolf!"

This time, no one paid any attention to him. Everyone went on working. They said, "Oh, we know your tricks. Leave us in peace and go back to tending your sheep."

The shepherd boy ran back to the meadow all by himself, only to find that the wolf had indeed had a good meal off his sheep. And that was the unhappy way he discovered that, if you tell too many lies, people won't believe you even when you are telling the truth.

THE FISHERMAN
AND HIS WIFE

THERE once lived a poor fisherman and his wife in a pigsty near the sea. Every day the man went out fishing. One day he was sitting on the rocks, where the water was very deep, hoping to catch some fish for supper. He sat with his fishing rod, staring down into the clear, calm water, catching nothing. Suddenly his line went down, down, down. When he pulled it up, he found he had hooked a very large flounder.

The flounder said to him, "Listen to me, Fisherman. I am no ordinary flounder, but an enchanted prince. What good would it do for you to eat me? Please put me back in the water."

"There is no need to say more. I certainly would not eat a fish that can talk!" said the fisherman. With that he threw the flounder back into the sea.

Then the fisherman went home to his pigsty.

His wife said, "Husband, didn't you catch anything today?"

The fisherman said, "I did catch one flounder, but he said he was an enchanted prince, so I let him go."

"Didn't you wish for anything first?" asked his wife.

"No," said the fisherman. "What should I have wished for?"

His wife said, "It is disgusting to live in this pigsty. You might have wished for a nice, clean little house for us. Go back and call that fish. Tell him we want a little house."

The fisherman did not really want to go, but he did not want to disagree with his wife, either, so he went back to the seashore. When he got there the water was not so clear and calm as before. He called,

> *"Flounder, flounder in the sea,*
> *Come, I pray thee, here to me.*
> *For my wife, good Ilsabil,*
> *Wills not as I'd have her will."*

Then the flounder came swimming to him and said, "Well, what does she want, then?"

"Ah," said the fisherman, "my wife says I should have wished for something from you. She does not like living in a pigsty. She wants a little house."

"Go, then," said the flounder. "She has it already."

When the man went home, the pigsty was gone. In its place stood a neat little house and garden. His wife was sitting on a bench outside the door.

"Look," she said. "Isn't this nice?"

"Yes," said the fisherman. "Now let us be happy with this."

"We will see," said his wife. Then they ate supper and went to bed.

Everything went well for a week or two. Then one day the woman said, "Husband, this little house is too small for us. Go to the flounder and ask him for a castle."

"Ah, Wife," said the fisherman. "This house is very nice. Why should we live in a castle?"

But his wife grew so angry when he questioned her that the poor fisherman had to go back to the sea again. Now the sea was rough, and the wind blew hard. The fisherman's heart grew heavy, and he said to himself, It is not right. All the same, he called,

> "Flounder, flounder in the sea,
> Come, I pray thee, here to me.
> For my wife, good Ilsabil,
> Wills not as I'd have her will."

The flounder came swimming through the rough sea and said, "Well, what does she want now?"

"Alas," said the fisherman, "she wants to live in a great stone castle."

"Go, then," said the flounder. "She is standing before the door."

When the fisherman got home, he found a great stone castle with many steps leading up to it. His wife was standing on the steps. She took him by the hand and said, "Come in."

When they entered the castle, they saw marble walls and many servants. There were crystal chandeliers and chairs and tables of silver. Fine food was on the table, and there was a stable full of horses and carriages. There was everything anyone could ever wish for.

"Look," said the wife. "Isn't this beautiful?"

The fisherman said, "Yes, indeed. Now let it be. We can live in this beautiful castle and never wish for anything again."

"We will see," said his wife, and they went to sleep in their castle.

Next morning the woman woke up early and looked out the window. She saw the countryside stretching for miles and miles. She poked her husband in the ribs and said, "Look at all that land. Wouldn't you like to be king over all that land? Go tell the flounder you wish to be king!"

"Ah, Wife," said the fisherman. "Why should I be king? I do not wish to be king."

"Well," said his wife, "if you won't be king, I will. Go to the flounder and tell him I wish to be king."

And the poor fisherman knew by the tone of her voice that she would not take no for an answer. So he went again to the sea and called,

> *"Flounder, flounder in the sea,*
> *Come, I pray thee, here to me.*
> *For my wife, good Ilsabil,*
> *Wills not as I'd have her will."*

This time the sea was very gray and stormy. The sky was dark with clouds, but the flounder swam up and said, "Well, what does she want now?"

"Alas," said the fisherman, "now she wants to be king."

"Go to her," said the flounder. "She is king already."

So the fisherman went home. When he came to the castle, it had grown much larger. It had two great towers and a guard at the door. Many soldiers were marching around with drums and trumpets. When he entered the castle, he saw his wife sitting on a high throne of gold and diamonds. A great gold crown was on her head, and a jeweled scepter was in her hand.

The fisherman went and stood before her and said, "Ah, Wife, now you are king."

"Yes," said his wife. "Now I am king."

"Now that you are king," said the fisherman, "let us wish for nothing more."

"No," said his wife. "I find the time passes very heavily. I can bear it no longer. Go to the flounder. I want to be emperor."

"Oh, Wife, why do you wish to be emperor?" said the fisherman. "I cannot ask that of the fish. There is only one emperor in all the land. I assure you, the flounder cannot make you emperor."

"What?" said the woman. "I am the king, and you are nothing but my husband. If I command you to go, then you must go!"

So the poor fisherman set out again for the sea. As he walked along, he said again and again to himself, This will not end well! This will not end well!

When he reached the sea, it was black and stormy. A harsh wind blew across the enormous waves. The fisherman was afraid. All the same, he called,

> *"Flounder, flounder in the sea,*
> *Come, I pray thee, here to me.*
> *For my wife, good Ilsabil,*
> *Wills not as I'd have her will."*

The flounder came swimming through the black water and said, "Well, what does she want now?"

"Alas, Flounder, my wife wants to be emperor," said the fisherman.

"Go to her," said the flounder. "She is emperor already."

So the fisherman went home. When he got there, the whole castle was surrounded with marble statues and formal gardens. Lords and ladies paraded through the great halls. The doors were made of gold. When the servants opened the door to the great hall, there sat his wife on a throne made of one piece of solid gold. She wore a jeweled crown that was so huge the fisherman could hardly see her face. She held her scepter in one hand. She held a crystal ball of the world in her other hand. On both sides of her stood soldiers with swords. Banners of embroidered silk waved in the air.

Her husband went and stood before her and said, "Wife, are you emperor now?"

And she said, "Yes, I am emperor now."

But a few days went by, and the woman again grew bored and restless and wished and wished for even more. One day she said, "Husband, go to the flounder! Tell him I want to be Pope!" And she shouted and stamped her foot and shook her scepter and the crystal ball of the world at her poor husband until he had no choice but to go and call the flounder once again.

This time the sea was blacker and stormier than the fisherman had ever seen it. His knees shook with terror as he called out,

> *"Flounder, flounder in the sea,*
> *Come, I pray thee, here to me.*
> *For my wife, good Ilsabil,*
> *Wills not as I'd have her will."*

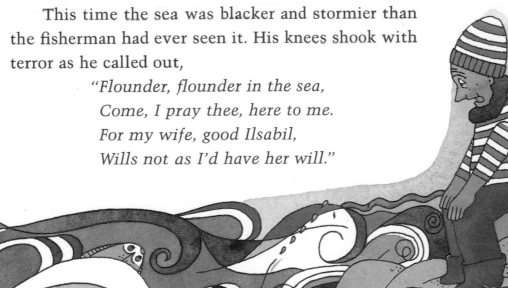

And the flounder looked up out of the wild waves and said, "Well, what does she want now?"

"Alas! Alas! This time she wants to be Pope!" said the fisherman.

"Go to her," said the flounder "She is Pope already."

When the husband got home he found his wife in robes of white satin, embroidered with gold and silver. All around her stood cardinals in caps and robes of scarlet. But the woman was still not satisfied.

That night when they went to bed, the fisherman's wife could not sleep. She tossed and turned, for she was trying to think of something even greater she could be.

At last the sun began to come up. When the woman saw the bright and rosy dawn and the golden sun in the sky, she sat straight up in bed. She poked her sleeping husband and said, "Husband! Wake up! Go to the flounder. Tell him I want to be able to command the sun and moon to rise. Tell him I want to be like God!"

The fisherman was so shocked by this that he tumbled out of bed onto the floor. He said, "Wife, what are you saying?"

"Husband," she said, "if I cannot make the sun and moon rise and set this very day, I shall not be able to bear it. Go at once! Tell that flounder my wish!" And she gave her husband such a terrible look that a shudder ran through him. Then she began to tear her hair and howl. That is how much she wanted to control the sun and moon.

So the fisherman pulled on his trousers and ran away like a madman.

Outside a terrible storm was raging. Rain and hail pelted him. Trees blew over in the wild wind. Mountains shook, and huge rocks tumbled into the sea. When the fisherman finally reached the sea, the sky was black as night. Thunder and lightning roared and flashed. The sea rolled in with foamy waves as high as church steeples.

The fisherman cried out, as loudly as he could,

> *"Flounder, flounder in the sea,*
> *Come, I pray thee, here to me.*
> *For my wife, good Ilsabil,*
> *Wills not as I'd have her will."*

Once more the flounder came and said, "Well, what does she want now?"

"Alas," said the poor fisherman, "she wants to be like God."

"Go to her," said the flounder. "You will find her back in the pigsty."

Immediately the sky turned blue. The sea became as calm and clear as it had been the day the fisherman first caught the flounder.

The fisherman went home. There was his wife, in their little pigsty. And they live there still.

BRIAR
ROSE

THERE once lived a king and queen who wished each day for a child. But they never had one.

One day, when the queen was swimming in the lake, a frog crept out of the water and said to her, "Your wish shall be fulfilled. Before a year has passed you will have a daughter."

What the frog said came true. Within a year a little girl was born to the queen. She was named Briar Rose because her cheeks were pink as roses. The king was so happy that he ordered a great feast. He invited all his friends, relatives, and acquaintances. He also invited twelve Wise Women so that they might grant good fortune to his child. There were thirteen Wise Women in his kingdom, but as he only had twelve gold plates for them to eat from, one of them had to be left out.

The splendid feast was held. When dinner was done, each of the Wise Women bestowed a gift upon the baby. One gave goodness, another gave beauty, a third gave riches, and so on. The Wise Women gave Briar Rose their great gifts until she had nearly everything in the world anyone could ever wish for.

When eleven of them had bestowed their gifts, suddenly the thirteenth Wise Woman entered the hall. She was very angry because she had not been invited to the feast. She spoke to no one but instead stared fiercely at all the guests. Then she waved her magic wand and cried out, "The king's daughter shall prick herself with a spindle and fall down dead when she is fifteen years old!"

Without saying another word, the angry Wise Woman spun around and left the room, slamming the door of the great hall behind her.

Everyone was shocked, and the queen began to cry. Then the twelfth Wise Woman, who had not yet given her good wish, said, "I cannot undo the evil spell, but I can soften it. It will not be death, but a deep sleep of one hundred years, into which the princess will fall."

The king wanted to keep this misfortune from happening to his dear child. So the next day he ordered that every spindle in the whole kingdom be burned.

As Briar Rose grew, the gifts of the Wise Women were more than fulfilled. She became so beautiful, modest, good-natured, and wise that everyone who saw her loved her.

It happened that on the very day when Briar Rose turned fifteen years old, the king and queen were not at home. The girl was left in the palace all alone. So she went around to all sorts of places, peeking into rooms wherever she wished. At last she came to an old tower. She climbed the narrow, winding staircase and reached a little door. A rusty key was in the lock. When she turned it, the door opened. There sat an old woman with a spindle, spinning flax.

"Good day," said the king's daughter. "What are you doing?"

"I am spinning flax," said the old woman.

"What is that thing that turns so cheerfully?" asked the girl, for she had never seen a spindle. As she said this she took hold of the spindle, wanting to spin, too. But she had scarcely touched the spindle when the thirteenth Wise Woman's wish came true.

Briar Rose pricked her finger with the spindle and collapsed upon a bed in the little tower room. Then she fell into a deep sleep.

And this sleep extended over the whole palace. The king and queen, who had just come home, fell asleep in the great hall. The horses fell asleep in the stable, the dogs in the yard, the pigeons on the roof, and the flies on the wall. The maid fell asleep in the kitchen. Even the fire that was flaming on the hearth became quiet and slept, and the roast meat stopped sizzling. The cook, who was just about to box the ears of the scullery boy because he had forgotten to do something, let him go, and they both closed their eyes and fell asleep exactly as they stood. The wind stopped blowing, and not a leaf on the trees in the palace courtyard stirred again.

All around the palace a hedge of thorns began to grow. Year after year it grew higher until at last nothing of the palace could be seen, not even the flag on the roof. The story of the beautiful sleeping princess, Briar Rose, spread all around the countryside. From time to time various kings' sons came and tried to get through the thorny hedge into the palace. But they always failed, so dense were the sharp thorns.

After many long years another king's son came to that country. He heard from an old man about the thorny hedge and the palace hidden behind it, and about the young princess who had been sleeping there for nearly a hundred years. He heard, too, of the many kings' sons who had tried and failed to get through the thorny hedge. But the young prince could not stop thinking of the beautiful princess who lay sleeping in the palace that was hidden by thorns. He made up his mind that, somehow, he would enter the palace and try to wake the princess from her sleep.

When he set out for the palace, the prince did not know that the spell was almost over, for the hundred years had passed. But as he came near the hedge of thorns, all the thorns turned into large and beautiful flowers that parted of their own accord and let him pass, unhurt.

In the stable and the courtyard he saw the horses and spotted hounds sleeping. On the roof sat pigeons with their heads tucked under their wings. When he entered the palace, he saw flies asleep upon the wall. The cook was still holding out his hand toward the scullery boy in the kitchen. The maid was sitting by the black hen she was about to pluck. In the great hall he saw the sleeping king and queen.

Then the prince went on still farther. It was so quiet in the palace that not a breath could be heard. At last he climbed up into the tower and opened the door to the little room where Briar Rose was sleeping. There she lay. She was so beautiful that the prince could not turn his eyes away. He knelt down and gave her a kiss.

As soon as he kissed her, Briar Rose opened her eyes and smiled at him sweetly.

Then they went down the stairs together. The king and queen awoke. The horses stood up and shook themselves. The hounds jumped up and wagged their tails. The pigeons on the roof pulled their heads out from under their wings and flew off into the countryside. The flies on the wall crept again, and the fire in the hearth blazed up and cooked the meat. The cook gave the scullery boy such a box on the ear that he howled out loud, and the maid finished plucking the hen.

Then the marriage of the prince and Briar Rose was celebrated with much joy and splendor, and they lived happily ever after.

MR. VINEGAR

THERE once lived a man and his wife who were very poor. They were so poor they lived in a vinegar bottle, and so they were called Mr. and Mrs. Vinegar. One day, when Mr. Vinegar was out, Mrs. Vinegar was sweeping the house. Suddenly an unlucky thump of her broom brought the whole house crashing down. She ran to find her husband.

As soon as she saw him she cried, "Oh, Mr. Vinegar! Mr. Vinegar, we are ruined! I have knocked the house down, and it is all in pieces."

Mr. Vinegar said, "My dear, let us see what can be done. Here is the door. I will carry it on my back, and we will go to seek our fortune."

They walked all day, and at night they entered a thick forest. They were both very, very tired, so Mr. Vinegar said, "My love, I will climb a tree, drag up the door, and you can follow me."

He did just that. Then they both stretched out on the door up in the tree and soon fell fast asleep.

In the middle of the night Mr. Vinegar was awakened by the sound of voices. To his horror and dismay he heard a band of thieves dividing up their loot. Mr. Vinegar could listen no longer. His terror was so great that he trembled and trembled. He trembled so much that he shook the door down upon the thieves' heads. The thieves ran away, but Mr. Vinegar did not dare come down from the tree until daylight. Then he scrambled down and lifted up the door. What did he see, under the door, but a pile of golden coins.

"Come down, Mrs. Vinegar!" he cried. "Our fortune is made! Come down, I say!"

Mrs. Vinegar got down as fast as she could, and when she saw the pile of money she jumped for joy.

"Now, my dear," she said, "I'll tell you what we must do. There is a fair in the nearest town. Take these golden coins and buy a cow. Then I can make butter and cheese to sell in the market, and we can live very comfortably."

Mr. Vinegar took the money, and off he went to the fair. When he got there he looked all around. At last he saw a beautiful red cow. It was an excellent milker and perfect in every way. So he bargained with the owner of the cow and bought it with all the golden coins.

By and by he saw a man playing the bagpipes. Everyone who heard him seemed to be giving him money.

Well, thought Mr. Vinegar, if I had those bagpipes I would be the happiest man alive, for my fortune would soon be made. So he went up to the man.

"Friend," he said, "what a wonderful instrument that is. What a great deal of money you must make!"

"Why, yes," said the man. "I make a great deal of money, to be sure, and it is a wonderful instrument."

"Oh!" said Mr. Vinegar. "How I would like to own it!"

"Well," said the man, "as you are a friend, I don't mind swapping it for that cow."

"Done!" said the delighted Mr. Vinegar. So the beautiful red cow was swapped for the bagpipes. Mr. Vinegar walked up and down and tried in vain to play a tune. No one put any pennies in his pocket. Instead, boys followed him, hooting, laughing, and pelting him with pebbles.

Poor Mr. Vinegar. His hands were cold. Just as he was leaving town he met a man with a fine, thick pair of gloves.

Oh, my fingers are so very cold! said Mr. Vinegar to himself. Now, if only I had those beautiful gloves, I would be the happiest man alive.

He went up to the man and said, "Friend, you have a fine pair of gloves there."

"Yes, truly I do," said the man. "My hands are as warm as can be on this cold November day."

"Well," said Mr. Vinegar, "I would like to have them."

"Well," said the man, "as you are a friend, I don't mind swapping them for those bagpipes."

"Done!" said Mr. Vinegar. He put on the gloves and felt perfectly happy as he walked along. At last he grew very tired. Then he saw a man with a good, stout walking stick coming toward him.

Oh, said Mr. Vinegar to himself. If only I had that stick, I would be the happiest man alive. He said to the man, "Friend, what a rare good stick you have."

"Yes," said the man. "I have walked many miles with this good stick. But if you have a fancy for it, I would be happy to swap it for that pair of gloves." Mr. Vinegar's hands were so warm and his legs so tired that he gladly made the swap.

As he grew nearer to the forest where he had left his wife, he heard a parrot calling his name. The parrot said, "Mr. Vinegar, you fool, you blockhead, you simpleton. You went to the fair and spent all your golden coins buying a cow. You weren't happy with a cow, so you swapped it for bagpipes you could not play, which were not worth one quarter of the money. You had no sooner got the bagpipes than you swapped them for gloves that were not worth one tenth of the money. When you got the gloves, you swapped them for a poor, miserable stick that you could have cut from any hedge."

At this the parrot laughed and laughed. Mr. Vinegar flew into a violent rage and threw the stick at the bird. The stick stuck in the tree, and he returned to Mrs. Vinegar without money, cow, bagpipes, gloves, or walking stick. I don't need to tell you that she gave him such a scolding that he never went off to the fair again.

THE
FROG
PRINCE

THERE was once a king whose youngest daughter was so beautiful that the sun itself was astonished whenever it shone on her face. Her father's castle was near a great, dark forest, and under an ancient tree in that forest, there was a well of deep, cool water. In the summertime the princess liked to go into the forest and sit beside the well. Her favorite plaything was a golden ball, which she loved to toss into the air and then catch in her hand. Day after day she spent many happy hours playing with her golden ball.

Now it so happened that, one day, the golden ball did not fall into her hand. Instead, it rolled away and fell down into the deep, cool water of the well in the great, dark forest. The king's daughter followed it with her eyes, but the golden ball quickly vanished, for the well was so deep that the bottom could not be seen. When this happened the princess began to cry.

She cried louder and louder, although there was no one there to comfort her.

Suddenly a voice said, "What is the matter, Princess? You are crying so hard that even a stone would show pity on you."

The princess looked around and saw a frog poking its big, ugly head out of the water.

"Ah, you old water splasher, is that you speaking?" said the princess. "I am crying because my golden ball has fallen into the well."

"Be quiet and stop crying," said the frog. "I can help you. But first, you must tell me what you will give me if I bring your plaything up to you."

"Whatever you want, dear frog," said the princess. "You may have my clothes, my pearls and jewels, and even the golden crown that I am wearing."

The frog answered, "I do not want your clothes, your pearls and jewels, or even your golden crown. I only want to be your friend. If you will let me sit next to you at the dinner table and eat off your golden plate and drink out of your golden cup and sleep on your satin pillow, then I will go down into the deep, cool waters of the well and bring up your golden ball. But first, you must promise me these things."

"Of course," said the princess. "I promise you everything you ask, if you will bring back my ball."

As she was saying this, though, she was thinking, What a silly frog! It is supposed to swim in the water and croak with the other frogs. It is not fit to be a friend to any human being!

The frog lowered its head into the water and sank down below the surface. Before long it came swimming up out of the deep water with the golden ball in its mouth. It rolled the ball onto the grass right next to where the princess sat. She was so delighted to see her pretty plaything once more that she picked it up and started to run home with it.

"Wait! Wait!" cried the frog. "Take me with you! I can't run as fast as you can!"

But it did no good for the poor frog to call out so pitifully, because the princess never looked behind her. Instead, she ran all the way home to the castle and forgot about the frog in the well who had brought her golden ball back to her.

The next evening, when the princess was at dinner with the king and all his court, eating from her golden plate, something climbed up the marble staircase of the castle with a *splish, splash, splish, splash*. When it reached the top of the stairs, it knocked at the door and called, "Princess, youngest princess, open the door for me."

The king's youngest daughter ran to see who was calling her. But when she opened the door and saw the frog sitting there, she slammed the door as hard as she could and ran back to the dinner table.

The king saw that she was very frightened, and he said, "My dear child, what has frightened you so?

Is there a giant outside the door who wishes to carry you away?"

"Ah, no," said the princess. "It is not a giant but a disgusting frog."

"Why is this frog at the castle? What does it want with you?" said her father.

"Yesterday," said the princess, "when I was in the forest playing by the well, my golden ball fell into the deep, cool water of the well. I cried so hard that the frog heard me and took pity on me and brought my ball up to me. But first, the frog made me promise it could be my friend and sit next to me at the dinner table and eat off my golden plate and drink out of my golden cup and sleep on my satin pillow. When I promised, though, I never thought that the frog would be able to come up to the castle and find me. Now, here it is, and it wants to eat with me!"

Just then, the frog knocked a second time, saying,
"Princess, youngest princess!
Open the door for me!
Do you remember the promise you made me
Yesterday by the cool waters of the well?
Princess, youngest princess!
Open the door for me!"

Then the king said to his daughter, "That which you have promised you must do. Go and open the door for the frog."

So the youngest princess went to the door and opened it. The frog came in and followed her with a *splish, splash, splish, splash* right to her chair. There it stopped and said, "Please lift me up beside you."

The princess hesitated, but the king commanded her to do as the frog asked. Once the frog was on the chair, it wanted to be on the table; and when it was on the table, it said, "Now push your little golden plate and your little golden cup closer to me so that we may eat and drink together."

Although the princess did this, it was easy to see she did not do it willingly. The frog enjoyed every bit of what it ate and drank. But the princess was so disgusted at having to eat with a frog, she almost choked on every mouthful she took.

At last the frog said, "I have eaten all that I want. Now I am tired. Please carry me to your room, so I may sleep on your little satin pillow."

The king's daughter began to cry, for she did not want even to touch the ugly frog who was asking to sleep on her own little satin pillow. And at this, the king grew angry at his daughter and said, "He who helped when you were in trouble ought not now to be despised by you."

So the princess took hold of the frog with two fingers, carried it upstairs, and put it in a dark corner. No sooner had she gotten into bed than the frog plopped across the room to where she was and said, "I am tired, too. I want to sleep as much as you do. Lift me up on your satin pillow, or I will tell your father."

At this, the princess grew terribly angry. She said, "I have let you eat off my little golden plate and drink out of my little golden cup. I have carried you up the stairs to my own room. But I will not let you sleep on my little satin pillow!"

Then the princess picked up the frog and threw it back across the room into the dark corner. "Now will you be quiet and let me sleep?" she said.

But when the frog landed in the dark corner, it was a frog no longer. Instead, it turned instantly into a handsome king's son with kind and beautiful eyes that looked as though they had known much sadness.

The prince told the princess how he had been bewitched by a wicked witch. He said that no one could have set him free from the spell of being a frog in the well but the princess herself. Then he asked her if she would come with him to his own kingdom and be his bride. She said yes, and her father told her she could go.

The next morning a carriage with eight white horses came driving up to take the young king's son and the princess far away to his kingdom. Each white horse wore white ostrich feathers on its head and was harnessed to the carriage with chains of purest gold.

Behind the eight white horses stood the prince's servant, Faithful Henry. When his beloved master had been turned into a frog, Faithful Henry had been so sad that he thought he would die. He had asked that three iron bands be placed around his heart, so it would not burst with grief.

Now Faithful Henry was filled with joy because the witch's terrible spell had been broken. He helped the young prince and princess into the carriage and climbed up behind the white horses, and they set out.

When they had driven just a short distance, the prince heard a cracking sound, as if something had broken. So he cried out, "Henry, our carriage is breaking!"

"No, Master," said Faithful Henry, "it is not the carriage. It is only an iron band that was around my heart."

Again and then again as they rode on their way, something cracked. And each time the prince thought the carriage was breaking. But it was only the iron bands springing from the heart of Faithful Henry because now his master was free and happy.

THE CAT ON
THE DOVREFELL

THERE was once a man way up in Finnmark who had caught a great white bear, which he was going to take to the king. He traveled and he traveled, leading the great white bear by a rope, until one night he came to a faraway and mountainous place called the Dovrefell.

Now, as it happened, the night was Christmas Eve. It was very cold and dark on the Dovrefell, and both the man and the great white bear were very, very tired. Not far off, in a deep valley at the foot of a high mountain, they saw a little cottage with lights burning brightly, so they walked up to it and knocked on the door. When the owner, whose name was Halvor, came to the door, the man said, "Could you give my bear and me a place to sleep tonight?"

Halvor said, "If only I could! But my wife and little children and I are just about to leave our cottage ourselves. Every Christmas Eve a pack of trolls comes down from the mountain and demands to stay in our cottage. They fight and squabble and make so much noise that we are forced to flee ourselves. So, you see, we don't have as much as a roof over our own heads for tonight, let alone one to share."

"Oh?" said the man with the great white bear. "If that is the only problem, you can surely lend us your house tonight. My bear and I are not afraid of trolls, and we are so tired we can sleep through anything."

Well, the man pleaded so hard that at last Halvor gave him permission to stay there. Before Halvor and his wife and children left, they set out a fine feast for the trolls. There were ginger cakes and rice pudding and smoked fish and fat sausages and black bread and warm milk and all sorts of good things to eat and drink. There was a blazing fire in the fireplace, too.

"If there is no feast ready for them," said Halvor, "the trolls will knock down every wall in the cottage. Oh, they are terrible beings, those trolls!"

As soon as Halvor and his wife and little children had left, the man went to sleep in the storeroom off the kitchen. The storeroom was quite empty because everything was on the table waiting for the trolls, so he had no trouble finding room for himself. As for the great white bear, it lay down to sleep under the stove in the kitchen.

Soon the trolls came down from the mountain. Some were big and some were small. Some had long tails and some had no tails at all. But all of them had noses as long as pokers, eyes as big as saucers, and long, matted hair. They began to fight over the food Halvor and his wife had set out for them. They were very greedy, and not one of them had any manners. They made a lot of noise with their squabbling and screaming and gobbling and slurping, too. But the man and the great white bear slept on. That is how tired they were.

Suddenly a little troll caught sight of the great white bear. He said, "Here's a big white cat sleeping under the stove." Then the troll took a fat, sizzling sausage and stuck it on a fork and poked it up against the great white bear's nose, screaming, "Here, kitty, won't you have some sausage?"

And when the little troll did this, the great white bear woke up. It was very angry at being awakened, and so it growled and roared and scared the trolls so much that they all, big ones and small ones, those with tails and those without, ran off screaming to the mountain they had come from. Then the great white bear went back to sleep.

The next morning Halvor and his wife and little children came back to their cottage just as the man and the great white bear were leaving. Halvor saw that not much of the feast had been eaten and that the trolls had not wrecked his cottage much at all. And Halvor thought about this for one whole year.

When Christmas Eve came again, he went out into the forest to cut wood for the holidays. While he was hard at work, he heard a voice in the forest calling, "Halvor! Halvor!"

Halvor knew it was one of the trolls calling him.

"Here I am," he answered.

"Have you still got your big white cat that sleeps under the stove?" said the troll.

"Yes, indeed, I have," said Halvor. "As a matter of fact, she is lying there right now, for she has just had seven kittens. And I can tell you, each one is bigger and fiercer than she is herself."

When he heard this, the troll began to howl and scream and tear his matted hair. He shouted angrily to Halvor, "Oh, if that is true, we can never come to visit *you* again!" Then the little troll ran off to the mountain where he belonged.

Never again did the trolls come to spend Christmas Eve in Halvor's little cottage on the Dovrefell. And that made Halvor and his wife and children very happy, indeed.

THERE was once a miller who had three sons. When he died, all he had to leave them were his mill, his donkey, and his cat. This small inheritance was quickly divided up. The oldest son took the mill, and the second took the donkey. All that remained for the youngest was Puss, the cat. The youngest was very disappointed in such a pitiful portion.

"My brothers," said he, "will be able to earn a decent living by combining what they have. As for me, as soon as I have eaten my cat and made a muff out of his fur, I will have to die of hunger."

Now Puss overhead these remarks. He said, very seriously, "There is no need for you to worry, Master. All you have to do is give me a leather drawstring pouch and a pair of sturdy boots, so I can walk through the underbrush. Then you will find that your portion is not so bad, after all."

The young man had often seen Puss using very clever tricks to catch rats and mice. So he thought there was some small hope that the cat could help him. Therefore, he gave him what he had asked for.

When he received the boots, Puss put them on. He hung the pouch around his neck and set off for a meadow where there were plenty of rabbits. He put some bran and lettuce in the pouch. Then he stretched out and pretended he was dead.

He was waiting for some young rabbit, who did not yet know the ways of this world, to come for the good food in the pouch.

He had hardly stretched himself out when things began to go as he wished. A foolish young rabbit darted into the pouch. Puss pulled the drawstring tight and caught it. Then he set out for the king's palace. He demanded to see the king and was shown to his private room.

Puss bowed low and respectfully before the king. "Sire," he said, "I bring you a rabbit from the Marquis of Carabas." This was the name Puss had given to his young master. "I have been told to present it to you on his behalf."

"Tell your master," said the king, "that I thank him and am deeply pleased by his thoughtfulness."

A few days later, Puss put some seeds in his pouch and hid himself in a wheat field. When two partridges fluttered into the pouch, Puss pulled the drawstring tight and caught them. He presented them to the king, just as he had the rabbit from the meadow. The king was no less appreciative than he had been before.

For months Puss went on in this way, bringing gifts in the name of the Marquis of Carabas. One day he learned that the king planned to take his beautiful daughter for a drive along the riverbank.

Puss went to his master and said, "If you will do as I tell you, your fortune will be made. You have only to go swimming in the river. Leave everything else to me."

The young man had no idea what Puss had planned, but he did as he was told.

As he was swimming in the river, the king's carriage drew near. Puss, who was standing on the riverbank, began to shout at the top of his voice, "Help! Help! The Marquis of Carabas is drowning!"

When the king heard Puss shouting, he stuck his head out the window of the carriage. He recognized the cat who had brought him so many gifts. He commanded his guards to go quickly and rescue the Marquis of Carabas.

While they were pulling the poor marquis from the river, Puss spoke to the king. He told the king that when his master was swimming, robbers had taken away his fine clothes. As a matter of fact, that rascal Puss had hidden them under a big stone. The king at once commanded the keepers of his wardrobe to go and select a suit of his finest clothes for the Marquis of Carabas.

The young man looked very handsome in such fine clothes. He looked so handsome that the king's daughter fell madly in love with him. So the king invited the Marquis of Carabas to come into his carriage and join him and his daughter on their drive.

Puss was overjoyed to see how splendidly his plan was working. He ran on ahead. Soon he came to some peasants who were mowing a field.

"Listen, good people who mow," said Puss. "If you do not tell the king that this field belongs to the Marquis of Carabas, you will be chopped up into sausage meat!"

When the king drove by, he asked the mowers whose field they were mowing. "It is the property of the Marquis of Carabas!" they all said at once. That was because Puss had frightened those people so with his threat.

"What a fine estate!" said the king to the young marquis.

"Thank you, Sire," said the Marquis of Carabas.

Puss ran on ahead until he came to some people threshing wheat. "Good people who thresh," said Puss. "If you do not tell the king that all this wheat belongs to the Marquis of Carabas, you will be chopped up into sausage meat!"

The king drove by a moment later. Again he asked who owned all the golden wheat he saw. The people were so frightened by the threat Puss had made that they all said, "It is the property of the Marquis of Carabas!" and the king was more pleased than ever.

Puss continued to run on ahead of the royal party. He made the same threat to everyone he met, so the king grew more and more impressed by the great riches of the Marquis of Carabas.

At last Puss came to a splendid castle that belonged to an ogre. He was a very rich ogre. All the lands they had passed through belonged to him. Puss had taken care to find out as much as he could about this ogre and what magic powers he possessed. Now he went to the door of the castle and asked to speak to the ogre.

The ogre received him as politely as an ogre can and asked him to sit down.

"I have been told," said Puss, "that you have the power to change yourself into any kind of animal. For example, I have heard that you can change yourself into a lion or an elephant."

"That is true," said the ogre. "Just to prove it, you will see me turn into a lion."

Puss was so frightened to see a lion in front of him that he scrambled up to the roof. This was difficult and dangerous for him, for his boots were no good for walking on roof tiles.

As soon as the ogre had turned into himself again, Puss climbed down. He admitted that he had been thoroughly frightened. Then he said, "I have also been told that you can turn into the smallest of animals. For example, I have heard that you can change yourself into a rat or a mouse. I confess that I find this impossible to believe."

"Impossible?" roared the ogre. "You will see!"

At that very moment he changed himself into a tiny mouse, which began to run around the floor. No sooner did Puss see the mouse than he pounced on it and ate it.

Presently the king came along. When he saw the ogre's splendid palace, he wanted to visit it. Puss heard the rumble of the carriage wheels as they passed over the drawbridge. He ran out into the court-yard just in time to greet the king.

"Welcome, Your Majesty, to the palace of the Marquis of Carabas!" he said, bowing low.

"What?" said the king. "Is this palace yours, also, my dear Marquis? I have never seen one more beautiful. May we go inside?"

The marquis gave his hand to the princess, and they followed the king as he climbed the stairs into the great hall of the palace. There they saw a magnificent banquet. It had been prepared for some friends of the ogre who had planned to visit him that very day. Of course, they all ran away when they saw that the king was there.

The king was delighted with the great wealth of the Marquis of Carabas. He also saw that his daughter loved the young man. So he said, "It is up to you, Marquis, whether you will become my son-in-law."

The marquis bowed very low and accepted the honor the king bestowed on him. He married the princess that very day.

Puss became a personage of great importance. Never again did he hunt mice, except for the fun of it.